My Time as Caz Hazard

Tanya Lloyd Kyi

orca soundings

ORCA BOOK PUBLISHERS

National Library of Canada Cataloguing in Publication Data

Kyi, Tanya Lloyd, 1973-
My time as Caz Hazard / Tanya Lloyd Kyi.

(Orca soundings)
ISBN 1-55143-319-2

I. Title. II. Series.

PS8571.Y52T54 2004   jC813'.6   C2004-904722-1

Summary: When Caz and Amanda's behavior seems to contribute to a
classmate's suicide, Caz must take a long hard look at her life.

First published in the United States, 2004

Library of Congress Control Number: 2004110933

Orca Book Publishers gratefully acknowledges the support for its
publishing programs provided by the following agencies:
the Government of Canada through the Department of Canadian
Heritage's Book Publishing Industry Development Program (BPIDP),
the Canada Council for the Arts, and the British Columbia Arts Council.

Cover design: Lynn O'Rourke
Cover photography: Christy Robertson

Orca Book Publishers	Orca Book Publishers
Box 5626, Stn B.	PO Box 468
Victoria, BC Canada	Custer, WA USA
V8R 6S4	98240-0468

07 06 05 04 • 5 4 3 2 1

Printed and bound in Canada.
Printed on 100% post-consumer recycled paper,
100% old growth forest free, processed chlorine free using vegetable, low VOC inks.

For Gordon and Shirley Lloyd

Acknowledgments

The author would like to thank Krystal Cullum for sharing her expertise in the areas of dyslexia and other learning disabilities.

Chapter One

I punched my so-called boyfriend at the end of grade ten.

Joel played for a junior hockey team, and his big dream was to get drafted and live in New York or Chicago. I thought he had two chances—slim and none—but that's not something you can tell your boyfriend.

Some nights, it seemed like Joel's main purpose was to bash into other players. They were always getting into fake fights, hauling off their shirts and throwing show-off punches. They pulled their fists back so fast they hardly touched each other.

I went to the games with my friend Mel—mostly for something to do. I would load us up with hot chocolates and popcorn, and Mel would do her best to look like a hockey fan. With her thick brown hair swept back and her metal-rimmed glasses, she looked more like a Hollywood starlet. I could picture her in one of those old black-and-white romance movies. Mel's too smart to be interested in hockey. She went to the games for my sake and watched with a slightly puzzled expression.

Once we saw a player get slammed against the boards near the stands. His head hit the Plexiglas and his eyebrow started bleeding, a little river of red curving down the side of his nose. He looked up and saw these teenyboppers pressed up against the other side of the glass and winked.

Mel made a disgusted sound. "He acts like he's their personal hockey god. And he's proud of that blood. It makes me sick."

"He is pretty good-looking. Without the blood," I grinned.

Joel wasn't hard to look at either. He had dark brown hair and wide shoulders and a little dusting of freckles that made him look like a kid when he smiled. We'd been going out for three weeks, so I'd been watching more hockey than usual.

Mel snorted again, still watching the bleeding guy. "The problem is that he knows he's good-looking. Can you believe those girls throwing themselves at him? Puh-leeze. They should receive immediate therapy for bad taste."

I almost choked on my hot chocolate. "Uh, Mel…have you forgotten that I'm dating a hockey player?"

She looked at me primly, but it was obvious that she had momentarily forgotten. "Maybe it doesn't count when you only date one. Just don't date more than three in a row."

"You're jealous," I teased.

"Wait until all of Joel's teeth get knocked out and then see how jealous I am. Next you'll be telling me that dentures are *so* sexy."

That was Friday night. On Monday morning I was talking to Mel before class and this bimbo from grade nine waltzed up to us. Her hair was teased into cutesy pigtails. She had a posse of two or three other girls standing behind her for moral support.

"I just thought you should know," she said. I hate it when people think you should know something. It's like when your parents say that something's for your own good. You can tell it's going to be bad.

Bimbo Girl took a deep breath. One of her little friends gave her a push forward. "Joel slept with me last night."

In the middle of her big sentence, her voice cracked. She turned and fled down the hallway and into the girls' bathroom. One of her friends stayed behind long enough to whisper, "She didn't know about you until afterward."

Mel tried to calm me down all morning.

"You should talk to him," she said, reasonably. "I'm sure he has an explanation."

"Yeah, like explaining that her breasts are bigger than mine."

Eventually, she gave up on me.

When the lunch bell rang, I went straight to the gym. I knew he'd be hanging out there with his hockey buddies. His back was to me. I walked up and tapped him on the shoulder. Everyone there went silent. They all must have known about Bimbo Girl. Anger swirled in my head until my eyes watered and my throat felt like it was closing.

Joel hardly had time to see me. My arm was already back as he turned around. I hit him smack in the nose. He fell flat on his back, like a tree. I turned around and left before he could say anything.

His friends were already laughing at him.

Chapter Two

I got suspended. Who knew? Two seconds, one punch and, voila—two weeks off.

At first it was totally worth it. It was the end of school anyway, so it was like getting an extra couple of weeks of summer vacation. My week of being grounded was over in a flash. (It was supposed to be two weeks, but my parents got lazy and stopped checking on me.) After that I took my sketchbooks and sat in the sunshine at the park almost every morning, drawing the kids who fed the pigeons, or the elderly couple that came and sat on the same bench every day.

Mel kept me up-to-date on the school gossip. Gossip like the week-long fling and subsequent breakup of Bimbo Girl and Puck Head. News of the split kept me happy for almost a month.

Then, at the end of August, everything fell apart. My old principal told my parents that I might do better in a different environment. That's how they all kept saying it—"different environment"—as if they were changing my pen at the zoo. My new school was Dogwood Senior Secondary in East Vancouver. It was smaller—only four hundred students—and supposed to be more supportive. "Supportive" turned out to mean anal. Before classes started, I had to go in for an entire day of tests. My parents and I were called in for a meeting the week after.

"We're late," Mom hissed as we swung open the double doors at the front of the school. Mom looked like she might be the new head of the parents' association. She had her blond hair (courtesy of Clairol) swept into some complicated bun on the top of her head. She's a realtor, and Dad says she scares people into buying houses. It might be true. Someone forgot to tell her that turquoise blue eye shadow went out of style about two decades ago.

"We're only ten minutes late," my dad said calmly as we filed toward the office. "They can't start without us."

Within a few minutes we were sitting on tweed chairs in a meeting room. The principal and the woman who gave me my tests—she turned out to be the learning assistance coordinator for the school district—sat together at the end of the table.

Test Lady cleared her throat. "Upon reading Caz's file, we had some concerns about her past performance at school."

Mom barely let her finish her sentence. "I assure you, the incident with that boy was a one-time occurrence. Caz has already been severely punished at home." I love how parents think being grounded is a severe punishment. As if watching soap operas and eating popcorn for lunch is somehow painful.

Test Lady waited for my mom to finish. "The violence is only one of our concerns. Some of the tests Caz wrote earlier this week show that she has a mild learning disability."

"She certainly does not," my mom said. Dad was silent.

"It's called dyslexia," Test Lady continued, as if Mom hadn't spoken. "I'm sure you've heard of it. Dyslexia is a congenital and developmental condition, with genetic and environmental causes."

I had no idea what she was talking about, and I could tell that Mom didn't understand her either. "That's ridiculous," she said.

"Symptoms include poor reading, writing and spelling skills," Test Lady said, "as well as some problems with mathematics."

That's where Mom walked out. She stood up with a huff and left the room. I looked at Dad to see if I should follow. He didn't move, so I stayed. After a minute he turned

9

to look at me. "Do you think that you might have this?" he asked me.

I shrugged. "I suck at English. Does that count?"

Test Lady nodded. "It does indeed. Mr. Hallard, Caz's dyslexia is not severe. What we would like to suggest is that you place her in our remedial reading program. She'll spend part of each morning with a small group of other students and receive personal attention from our learning assistance teacher. For the remainder of the day, she can take regular classes."

Dad agreed to everything, like he always does, and I tuned out. Was dyslexia curable? I didn't want to ask.

When we got outside, Mom was in a fury. "I can't believe you stayed and let that woman talk to you like that," she shouted as soon as Dad climbed into the car.

"She's only trying to help," Dad said.

Mom echoed him in a high voice. "She's only trying to help. Well, Ms. Goody Two-Shoes can stuff it. Caz isn't stupid. I hope you told her that!"

"I told her that we would do whatever it takes to help Caz improve," Dad said. I thought that was nice of him, although I saw no real hope of improving.

"You are so immensely spineless," Mom snarled. At Dad, not me. "They probably thought 'sucker' the minute they saw you. They can put your daughter into whatever retard class they want, and you say nothing."

I sank into the backseat upholstery and pretended I wasn't there.

"No one's calling Caz a retard," Dad said.

"No one says retard anymore," I told them. That was a mistake. It gave them an excuse to stop yelling at each other. They both glared at me instead.

When we got home I went straight to the phone to call Mel and tell her how horrible Mom had been. Then I realized that I'd have to explain about the remedial reading class. Halfway through dialing, I hung up.

Chapter Three

On the first day of school at Dogwood, I wore a burgundy skirt with my high black boots. A bit sleazy, I guess, but I wanted to make an impression. And I succeeded. I wasn't even in the hallway for two minutes before this guy with curly black hair and huge brown eyes separated himself from his friends. I could tell he was the type who stopped conversation at a party just by entering the room.

"New kid?" he asked. I told him I'd just transferred.

"I'm Brad. I'll show you around."

"You could show me to my first class," I told him, giving him my best flirty look. I reached in my bag for the schedule the principal had given me. I found it, already crumpled. "It's 112."

"Sure," he said, "112." Then all of a sudden he stopped talking. His eyes looked like they were scanning the hallway for an escape route. Was it my imagination? Had I developed a giant zit on my forehead in record time?

"I just remembered something," he said. "I gotta go. Your class is at the end of the hall."

The door was only a few steps ahead and I found it easily enough. As I was walking into the classroom, I heard a guy's voice at the other end of the hall calling, "Check it out—a new sped!" I glanced in that direction. Brad and his friends were looking straight at me, leering.

I ducked into the classroom as if it were an emergency shelter. Then I looked around.

This couldn't possibly be the right place. It looked more like a day care than a high school classroom. There were two bulletin boards covered with brightly colored construction paper, looking like they were ready to showcase new finger paintings, and there was an alphabet pinned to the top of one wall.

Seated around a long, rectangular table were four other kids — two girls on one side and two guys on the other. One guy was rocking back and forth slightly, tapping on the table. He had blond hair that hung over his forehead and swayed back and forth into his eyes as he rocked. He didn't look up. The other guy had dark skin and piercing black eyes. He was staring at me like I'd just killed his best friend. It made me want to shiver.

I closed my eyes. Please, please, please let this be the wrong classroom. I looked back at the open door. The number was definitely 112. I scanned the two girls on my side of the table. The first one looked like she was dressed in her grandmother's sofa, so I chose a chair beside the prettier one.

"What's a sped?" I asked her, ignoring Psycho Boy's continued stare.

She rolled her eyes. "Special education student," she enunciated, giving me a clear view of her bubble gum. "Welcome to Dogshit Secondary. You can ignore Jaz over there. He's brilliant—shouldn't even be here—but he's dealing with, like, serious anger management issues." I jumped as Jaz—Psycho Boy—scraped his chair back a fraction and transferred his glare. The girl with the bubble gum didn't flinch.

She held out her hand for me to shake. It was adorned with spiky silver rings in gothic designs. "I'm Amanda. What nuts-for-brains called you a sped?"

"Some guy named Brad."

"Looks like he just flew his private jet from Hollywood?" she asked.

I nodded.

"Well, don't stress about it. It's not like he's getting into Harvard any time soon. He's the biggest dealer in the school."

"Drugs?" I said, trying not to look shocked. He'd seemed more like an art dealer than a drug dealer.

Amanda winked at me. "It's not the worst thing in the world. I wouldn't run the other way if he asked me out. Can't blame me for that, can you?"

I didn't have time to answer before our teacher swept into the room. She had crazy hair that was flying in all directions and she wore a long skirt and a crystal necklace on a brown leather cord.

"Talk about a flashback to the hippie era," Amanda muttered under her breath.

The teacher was also wearing what looked like a Girl Guide vest, several sizes too small. It was covered in those little badges they award for baking cookies or starting a fire. I wouldn't know — I quit Brownies after three weeks. I couldn't handle all those sucks in one room singing about owls.

"I'm Ms. Samuels." When she smiled, her eyes crinkled in the corners and she looked like we were her favorite people in the world. "We're going to be spending lots of time together, so why don't we get to know each other. How about we share our names and our favorite hobbies?"

Amanda made gagging sounds.

"Why don't you start, dear?" Ms. Samuels said, her smile fading.

This time Amanda cleared her throat and crossed her hands on the desk in front of her, like a model student. "I'm Amanda. I like sunsets, long walks on the beach and kittens," she simpered.

Ms. Samuels nodded as if Amanda were serious. "Next?" she said, turning to me.

"Caz. I like…" My brain suddenly went blank. "Shopping," I finally stuttered.

When it was Jaz's turn, I'm pretty sure he said "go to hell" under his breath. Ms. Samuels pretended not to hear.

"Rob?" she said. Apparently she was talking to the rocking kid, but he didn't answer.

"He's what they call 'non-verbal,'" Amanda whispered to me. "About as chatty as the sphinx."

Finally Ms. Samuels turned to the third girl, the one dressed in upholstery, who spoke so quietly I could barely hear her. "My name's Dodie and I like sewing," she whispered.

Amanda made gagging sounds again.

"Good," Ms. Samuels said, ignoring Amanda. "Now, you're probably wondering why I'm wearing this vest. A few of you are having some difficulty with spelling, and we're going to begin the year by reviewing the rules. We'll start with the consonant sound 'dge,' as in badge."

This time when I looked at Amanda she seemed to have dropped into a coma, and I understood completely. A year of spelling sounded like death by slow torture. And did Ms. Samuels think we were in preschool? As she unfolded a poster of the Golden Gate Bridge — another "dge" sound — I slid down in my seat and kicked Amanda under the table. When she turned, I showed her the first page of my notebook.

I'd written: Time to jump off a le<u>dge</u>.

Chapter Four

My work with Ms. Samuels was going to count as English for the first semester, so the remainder of my day was divided into three. There was history, with the oldest teacher known to man. He taught while clinging to a podium at the front of the class, as if he might topple if he lost his grip.

After that came math, which I did my best to sleep through, and art. The art teacher was also old, but he looked less likely to croak in the near future.

"And who are you, young lady?" he asked when I sat down. He removed old-fashioned spectacles to look at me more closely.

"Caz Hallard," I said, digging my sketchbook out of my bag.

"Hmm…obviously a Virgo," he said.

The rest of the class giggled, but I looked up at him in surprise. He hardly seemed the type to study astrology. And he was right — my birthday was in September.

"Nice people, Virgos," he mused as he sauntered back to the front of the class. "Organized, too."

I looked at my sketchbook suspiciously, as if it had given away my secrets. Then Mr. Spectacles started drawing on the board. With only a few strokes, he outlined a method of showing perspective in an illustration. A farmyard fence seemed to slowly disappear into a background of rolling fields.

Bending my head, I hastily copied the example into my book. He might have been strange, but at least he knew how to draw.

Amanda found me at my locker after school. "So. Shopping," she said, snapping her gum. I hoped it wasn't the same piece she'd been chewing that morning.

"What?"

"Shopping. You said that was your thing."

"I guess. I couldn't think of anything else to say."

"Want to go to the mall?" she asked.

I didn't really want to go. I wanted to race home and call Mel and whine about how hellish my new school was (except for art). But I didn't want to say no to Amanda, the only person who had actually talked to me all day.

"Sure. The mall sounds great."

It was only a couple of blocks away. It was filled with winter clothes, even though it was only the first week of September. We wandered through one of the department stores.

"Hey, check it out," Amanda called, holding up a purple paisley skirt, tightly pleated. "It was made for you. Seriously." It looked like something my great-aunt might wear.

I smirked at Amanda. "I was thinking of trying this on instead," I said, grabbing a hideous sequined blouse from the rack.

Just then a saleswoman appeared — the condescending kind who thinks she owns the store. "Perhaps you girls are looking for the junior miss section on the second floor?" she said, pressing her lips into a prim red bow.

We both dumped our clothes on the nearest racks. I was ready to slink away, but Amanda looked up at the woman and batted mascara-clotted lashes.

"I was going to buy that for my mom's birthday. But then I saw the hanger up your ass and I changed my mind," she said. Grabbing my elbow, she waltzed us toward the door.

I turned to call over my shoulder. "You have lipstick on your teeth!"

Once in the mall, we collapsed onto a bench in a fit of giggles.

"Did she really have lipstick on her teeth?" Amanda gasped when she could breathe well enough to talk.

"No. But I wanted to say something mean and I couldn't think of anything."

That sent Amanda into another giggle fit. "You're right," she said.

"About what?"

"Shopping's perfect. And I have another idea. See the dollar store over there?"

I nodded.

"Do you think you can cause a distraction when we go in there?"

"What kind of distraction?" I felt my cheeks going red just thinking about it.

"I don't know. Complain about something you bought last week."

"What are you going to do?" I asked.

Amanda just grinned. Not waiting to see if I was going to agree, she strolled casually into the store and started browsing.

I followed reluctantly. What could I complain about? Especially at a dollar store. The clerk was going to tell me to shut up and spend another dollar on something new.

When I got there, the clerk was busy anyway. There were two plump women in front of him, making him add up their bill a second time.

"Those wrapping paper rolls were on special," one of them was saying.

I heard a hiss from between the shelves. "Hurry up," Amanda whispered.

Looking around frantically, I spotted a stack of cheese graters near the edge of a shelf. I nudged them and they crashed to the floor. The women and the clerk stopped talking and stared at me.

"I'm so sorry," I stuttered. "They just slipped. I'll put them back…" The three of them kept looking, not saying anything, until I'd replaced the graters. I couldn't see Amanda so I ducked out the door.

I spotted her a few stores down, loitering in front of a shoe display. "Come on," she motioned.

She led the way outside. When we got to the middle of the parking lot, she reached in her coat pocket and pulled out four chocolate bars. "Here's your half of the hot goods," she grinned, handing me two.

"You stole these?"

"We stole these," she said happily.

I looked behind us, as if there might be a team of security guards on our trail.

"They're only chocolate bars. Relax," Amanda said.

I nodded and slipped them into my pocket. Who was going to miss a few chocolate bars? It wasn't like the store was going to go bankrupt.

Chapter Five

When I got home I could hear my mom banging drawers open and closed upstairs. My dad called me into the living room, where my little brother was already waiting. Ted was in grade nine and pretty cool in an obsessed-with-multimedia kind of way. He was holding his video game controller, but the TV was turned off. He looked wary, as if Dad were about to send him to boarding school in Siberia.

"What's up?" I asked, climbing over the arm of the sofa to sit cross-legged beside Ted. As a general rule, I avoided sitting on the sofa. It was sort of a silent protest. We used to have a big chocolate-colored couch like a velvet mud pit, waiting to suck you in. Old and ugly, but unbelievably comfortable. Then Mom started reading home décor magazines and bought this "camelback sofa." It was called that because there was a hump along the back. It was also about as comfortable as sitting on a camel.

So I usually avoided the sofa. This time the disadvantages were outweighed by the advantages of sitting by Ted—he hated it when I sat too close to him. Surprisingly, he didn't complain.

Dad took a deep breath. "Your mom and I have been having some problems lately," he said.

"And the Oscar for understatement of the century goes to…" I said dramatically. No one laughed. Ted studied his video game controller.

"We're going to try living separately for a while," Dad continued.

27

This time I stared at him in silence.

"Maybe you were expecting this," Dad mused.

Suddenly my brain clicked back into action. "Wait! Who's we? Who's living separately?" I asked. Ted remained silent.

"Your mom has rented an apartment downtown. She has an extra bedroom, so you can stay with her whenever you want. But I hope you'll want to continue to live here, with me."

Clang! Ted threw his controller onto the glass coffee table, which vibrated with the impact. He kicked the cord out of his way and scuffed out of the room, hauling up his pants as he went. Dad waited until he was gone, then turned to me with a sigh.

"This has nothing to do with you," he said.

"Obviously, since you've decided everything without even telling us."

"We thought if we had a plan in place, the transition would go more smoothly for you kids." He sounded completely calm, as if we were transitioning from one brand of breakfast sausage to another.

"You both suck." Not the most impressive thing to say. It was the best I could do on short notice.

"Mel phoned yesterday and today," he said, still calm. "You should call her."

"Whatever." I followed Ted.

I could hear my mom still banging around. When I poked my head through the doorway, it was like being sucked into a disaster zone. The closet had obviously been hit the hardest—hangers dangled empty, sweaters hung half off their shelves and socks littered the floor. The bed was covered in suitcases.

I took a step inside and Mom finally noticed me. I don't know what I was expecting. Waiting for Mom to apologize is like waiting for the polar ice caps to melt—scientifically possible but unlikely in the near future. A couple of months ago she turned an entire load of my white laundry bright pink, and all she did was shrug and say, "Mmm…bad luck. You're old enough to do your own laundry, anyway."

This time, when she turned her head toward me, her hands kept working.

"Your dad talk to you?"

I nodded. I guess I must have looked mad, because her jaw set the way it does when she's refusing to extend my curfew.

"It's hardly the end of the world. You're just going to have to adjust."

"Whatever," I shrugged.

"Get me some newspapers from the recycling bin downstairs, will you? I need more packing material."

When I turned to go, my eyes slid past the dresser, a jumble of keys, lipsticks, mints and a fifty-dollar bill. Without looking back at Mom, I whisked the bill off the surface and stuffed it in my pocket. I don't know why. It wasn't like I usually stole money from my parents. This time, it seemed like she owed me something.

Ignoring Mom's newspaper request, I made for Ted's bedroom. There was no answer when I knocked, so I slowly pushed the door open. He was sitting on the end of the bed, bouncing a basketball off the opposite wall. His headphones were on, the music playing so loudly that I could hear a garbled version of it from the doorway. I walked over and flicked one of his ears. He jumped.

"What do you want?" he grumbled, turning down the music only slightly.

"To see if you're okay."

"Perfect," he said.

"I thought you might want to talk."

"Did you know that at the Sydney Olympics, Vince Carter slam-dunked the ball over the head of a guy who was more than seven feet tall?"

"That's thrilling." My twisted brain couldn't remember how to spell, but Ted could remember years of basketball facts. Genetics were totally unfair. "You're changing the subject," I told him.

"We weren't talking about a subject." Welcome to the world of little brothers. They're entirely annoying. I suddenly remembered the chocolate bars I had in my pocket. I pulled one out and threw it on the bed beside him.

"Where did this come from?" he asked.

"I stole it," I said, trying not to sound too pleased with myself.

"You did not."

"I did."

"I don't want it then." He tossed it back toward me and I let it fall on the floor as I left. Ted was still throwing the basketball at the wall. I saw a flash of the future — one Hallard kid becomes a famous TV sportscaster. The other ends up illiterate, unemployed and enormous from eating stolen chocolate bars.

Chapter Six

We progressed to the "sh" sound in Ms. Samuels' class.

Her blank box of a classroom was starting to show traces of our existence. There were the badges pinned in one corner, around the Golden Gate Bridge poster. A couple of days before, she had hung clouds from the ceiling in celebration of "cl." She'd even posted this crazy picture of a stripper that Amanda drew to represent "str."

We were also learning rules of spelling that applied to all sorts of words. It was actually kind of cool, when I could remember the rules. For example, when a one-syllable word had a short vowel sound, the end consonant was always doubled. There was a trick to help remember that one—"Buzz off, Miss Pill."

When I got to class, Rob and Dodie were the only ones there. Dodie was sitting with her collage— our latest homework assignment in the "sh" category—displayed in front of her. I could see she had done it wrong. She had potato chips in it. As if they were spelled "potato ships." Of course, it was probably hard to think while wearing such hideous clothes.

"Nice cardigan."

"Thanks," she whispered, without looking up from the table.

"Do you buy your own clothes?"

She shook her head.

I started to suggest that she ask for an allowance, but Amanda swooped in.

"Caz Hazard and Dodie Doorknob, you both look smashing this morning," she chirped, exaggerating the "sh" sound in "smashing."

"My last name's Hallard," I told her.

"I like Hazard," she said. "As in hazard to your health." At that moment she spotted Dodie's collage on the table.

"Did you actually do that piece of crap assignment? I've never heard of something so stupid. I swear that woman thinks we're in kindergarten."

"No, that woman doesn't," Ms. Samuels said from behind Amanda as she entered the classroom and closed the door behind her.

Amanda didn't even flinch. She just smirked.

A second later, Ms. Samuels was the one to flinch as the door banged open. Jaz slammed it shut again behind him and dropped into a chair. He pulled a rolled-up piece of paper from the inside pocket of his jean jacket and flicked it onto the table. As far as I could tell, the only thing glued to it was a giant picture of a turkey. I couldn't help grinning.

I had kind of liked doing the collage. My mom decided to pick up some more things for her new apartment the night before, so cutting up magazines was a good escape from the sounds of moving furniture. I found a woman's shoulder. (The poor *Cosmo* model never even saw my scissors coming.) I added pictures of a cruise ship and seashells and snipped a tiny piece of our living room shag rug.

Ms. Samuels picked up Dodie's collage from the table. "This is very good, Dodie," she smiled. "I like your use of color." I rolled my eyes. It was obvious Ms. Samuels couldn't think of anything else nice to say.

"Caz? Did you finish your collage?"

As Ms. Samuels spoke, Amanda turned to look at me. Her raised eyebrows said, "Don't desert me now."

I shook my head. "Didn't get it done," I said.

Ms. Samuels looked disappointed for a moment. "Maybe by tomorrow," she said. Then she turned to the blackboard and began the class.

When we left the room at noon, I made sure Amanda and Jaz both left before me. Then I dropped my collage facedown on the table. It wasn't really like handing it in.

I finished my lunch early and headed for my locker, thinking that I could grab my sketchbook and put some finishing touches on my work before class.

It was pouring outside. The hallways were so crowded that I had to elbow my way through. When I finally got close to my locker, I found drug-dealer Brad and a group of his friends in my way. I tried to skirt around them, but no luck.

"Sped alert," I heard one of them say.

"Hey, it's Caz, right?"

I looked up, surprised to see Brad speaking to me.

"Want to go out with me some time?"

It wasn't like I was going to say yes. Not even if the universe was about to end and Brad and I were the only hope for the survival of the species. But when a guy like Brad suddenly asks you out, your jaw automatically drops. Then the entire circle of guys erupted in laughter.

"Go out with a sped! Nice one, Brad!" They were slapping him on the shoulder as if he were a stand-up comedian. Feeling my face turn more and more red, I backed away through the crowd and headed for the girls' washroom.

Amanda found me just as I got there. I swiped the tears from the edges of my eyes, not wanting to explain what happened. She didn't notice. Instead, she pulled me into the bathroom with her as the bell rang.

"Hey, Hazard, come and hang out with me," she whispered. "I can't stand the thought of going to math today. If that guy makes me do ratios one more time, I'm going to dip myself in oil and light a match. Really. I'm going to wrap myself in foil and throw myself into a deep freeze. I'll take…"

"Okay, okay. I get it," I stopped her, laughing. "I'm not exactly in the learning mood either."

I sat at one end of the bathroom counter while Amanda perched on the other. She tugged off one sock and balanced her foot on the edge of a sink, pulling nail polish from her purse.

"What do they do when you skip out?" I asked her.

"Who?"

"The school. Do they send notes home or something?"

Amanda shrugged. "If they do, they probably send them to the wrong address. I changed foster homes twice this summer."

"You're in foster care?"

"Don't look so shocked. I'm not the only one. Even Dodie Doorknob's a foster."

My eyes widened. "Why?"

"Her mom's psychotic or something. Aren't they all?"

Thinking of my mom's behavior lately, I was inclined to agree.

Amanda launched into stories about her new foster sister, who kept sneaking out of the house at night. After a while I tuned out. I started writing on the mirror with my finger, watching the lines appear and disappear.

"Skipping out," I wrote. Then, "Caz HAZARD." When I turned back to Amanda, she was dabbing lipstick on her lips, then smearing it around with lip-gloss.

"Want some?" She tossed me the lip-stick tube.

I opened it and turned to the mirror again. "Dodie Doorknob," I wrote in big pink letters. It seemed childish. After a minute I added, "does Dogwood." It wasn't any less immature, I admit, but I thought Ms. Samuels would be proud of my consonant use.

"Executed with true creative flair," Amanda grinned, hopping off the counter to give me an elaborate bow. "Now let's blow this Popsicle stand."

We padded out through the deserted hallways, past the stoners smoking along the school fence and toward the mall again. It was windy and the air blew through my sweater, chilled my skin and sent my hair flying over my face. I suddenly felt carefree, as if the worst had already happened. I was already skipping out. I'd already written mean things on the mirror. What else could I possibly get in trouble for?

When we got to an accessories store, I nudged Amanda. "This time you provide the distraction," I said. Then I strolled inside and began trying on scarves, checking myself out in the mirror each time.

I heard Amanda yelp. "Ouch! Okay, you've got to help me," she whined to the clerk. "I tried this ring on and it won't come off."

With a quick snap I tugged the tags off a silky red scarf and shoved it down the front of my sweater. Then I walked right past Amanda and the saleswoman, glancing at them as if casually curious. Amanda now had oil on her finger, and the ring was sliding slowly off.

She met me outside, as before.

Exhilaration coursed through me. "I can't believe I did that," I squealed. We were just tapping our fists together in congratulations when a man stepped up behind us.

"Excuse me, girls," he said. I turned just enough to see a hint of a paunch, a black leather belt, a blue shirt. Without waiting to hear more, without even glancing at each other, Amanda and I started running.

"Hey! Stop! You girls come back..." his booming voice bounced through the half-empty mall after us. We didn't stop. We didn't stop until we were two blocks away. Then we collapsed on a bus stop bench.

"Was he a security guard?" I gasped.

"I don't know. I think he was wearing a radio," Amanda said.

"Maybe he was just some guy who wanted to ask the time."

"I don't think so."

"But he didn't chase us," I said.

Amanda started laughing. "He might have had a heart attack. I could hardly keep up with you. Did you run track in a past life or something?"

As I caught my breath and started to relax again, I remembered the scarf inside my sweater. I pulled it out slowly, like a magician pulling handkerchiefs from his sleeve. It seemed even brighter in the sunshine. It would look great on Mel, but I hadn't exactly been seeing her much since I switched schools. When I remembered Ted's reaction to the chocolate bar, I decided against offering it to her.

"It's gorgeous," raved Amanda.

I shrugged. "Red looks terrible on me. Might look good on you, though."

I wrapped it loosely around her neck. "Was it worth the run?" I asked.

She smiled. A real smile, not her usual smirk. "Definitely."

Chapter Seven

I got home late and found Ted sitting on the floor of the kitchen, eating handfuls of cereal out of the box. A dusting of broken flakes covered his baggy sweatshirt. Not exactly a fashion statement.

He was smarter than he looked, though. Lately he'd been proofreading my homework for me. On Ms. Samuels' advice, I'd asked him to circle any errors in pencil, but not correct them. Then I would go through and fix everything, erasing his pencil marks as I went. For a grade nine kid, he had pretty good spelling.

From his slouch on the floor, he motioned me to silence and pointed to the vent above him. We could hear voices echoing down from the upstairs bedroom. I sank down beside him and helped myself to a handful of his cereal.

"That's pure stupidity," came my mom's muffled shout.

"I simply assumed," my dad said.

That's how my mom and dad fought. Mom yelled and Dad answered in his I'm-so-much-more-reasonable-than-you voice. A voice that obviously made Mom even more angry.

"Well, you can unassume. You're an unmotivated lump. You can barely pay for their food, let alone their education. I can't believe you would even consider..."

"What are they talking about?" I whispered to Ted.

"Us."

"What?"

"They're talking about which one gets to keep us," he mumbled.

"I thought we were staying here!" I said, forgetting to whisper for a minute.

Ted put a finger to his lips. "So did I. So did everyone except Mom, apparently. She says she has an extra bedroom in her apartment for us."

"There is no way I'm sharing a bedroom with you," I told him.

"It's not like I want your putrid perfume in my bedroom," he said, "but no one's asking us."

"We'll see about that." Leaving him cramming more cereal into his mouth, I stomped my way upstairs. I tried to make extra noise to warn them, but when I got to the hallway I could still hear them yelling at each other. I swung open their bedroom door without knocking.

"What do you call having the same job for ten years?" my mom was yelling. "That warehouse is going to kill you one of these days."

"Hello? Earth to alien parents? I thought that since you're involving the whole neighborhood in this fight, you might want to consult your kids."

They barely looked at me. "Go to your room," my mom said.

"Ted and I aren't moving."

This time my mom took a step toward me. "Mind your own business," she said.

"That makes no sense. How can you even say this isn't my business?"

I could see her gritting her teeth. For a minute I thought she was going to scream at me. Instead she held her voice to a hiss. "Go to your room, shut the door and stay there until someone asks for your opinion. Which they probably won't."

I left then, slamming the door behind me. Then I went to my room and slammed that door, too. "Bitch," I said aloud to the empty room. I wasn't sure who I was madder at —my mom for being so mean, or my dad for not defending me. If he wasn't such a wimp, maybe we wouldn't be in this mess.

My mom and dad had been having the exact same fight about twice a year since I could remember. Probably since before I was born. My dad was on his twentieth year in shipping and receiving. He liked it. He said he was good at it.

The fight went like this: Mom would see another job in a newspaper ad and cut it out for my dad. Dad would ignore it. Mom would tell him to apply. Dad wouldn't. Mom would say he had no interest in providing for his family. Dad would say he provided just fine and not to worry so much.

My mom's idea of providing and my dad's idea of providing were two different things. Maybe because of all those home décor magazines my mom read. A couple of years ago, I guess she gave up on him. She got her real estate license and started selling houses. She was good at it, too. Better than she was at ironing and making lunches. She was never exactly Betty Crocker material.

There was a soft knock at my door and Ted poked his head in.

"Nice going," he said softly.

"Yeah. Thanks a lot."

"So I guess we're moving?"

"Dad's never won a fight in his life. What do you think?"

In the morning, I woke up aching to see Mel — someone who knew me so well that I could completely relax. Suddenly all the reasons I hadn't called her seemed trivial. It wasn't like she was going to interrogate me about my new classes. I didn't have to tell her about Ms. Samuels and remedial reading. Unless I wanted to.

I called her before I left the house, and she agreed to meet for coffee after school. Of course, everything went wrong from the start. For instance, I couldn't stop at my locker without bumping into Amanda, and I couldn't bump into Amanda without inviting her along.

I knew they wouldn't like each other. The minute I introduced them I could see Mel taking in Amanda's black eyeliner and chunky earrings. I held my breath, waiting for Amanda to make some snide comment about Mel's brand-name jeans. She didn't, though. Instead she tagged along quietly until we reached the door to the coffee shop.

"Coffee's so boring. Let's go somewhere interesting. Come on."

Before Mel could protest, the two of us were in tow down the block, then into a back alley. I was about to ask where we were going when Amanda ducked into a doorway. A vivid hand-painted sign on the wall above read "Tally's Tattoo Parlor."

"She can't be serious," Mel said, stopping dead.

I grinned at her. "We might as well look. They can't force-tattoo us or anything."

Inside, a hulking guy with his arms covered in tattoos and his hair dyed purple leaned across the counter. I assumed that this was Tally.

"You lookin' at your options again?" he asked Amanda.

Ignoring him, Amanda waved us over to the sample designs on the wall. "This is the one I'm getting. It's going to take three visits — one for the black outline, one for the purple scales and one for the orange.

It's going to stretch from my shoulder blade to just below my waist." She pointed to a winged dragon with stylized black flames issuing from its jaws.

"Lovely," was all that Mel said.

"I need almost three hundred bucks just to get it started," Amanda mourned.

Grinning, I offered the fifty-dollar bill still in my wallet.

"Where did you get that?" she gaped.

"Courtesy of my mom's dresser. Which isn't actually her dresser anymore, since she's moving out."

Now it was Mel's turn to gape. "Your mom's moving out?"

I could tell she was mad that I hadn't told her. Luckily I was saved by Tally the tattoo man leaning even farther over the counter. "Fifty bucks will get you a nice belly button ring," he said, raising one pierced eyebrow for emphasis.

"Hah!" Mel said, like it was the most ridiculous idea in the world.

That's what made me do it, I think. Ten minutes later I was lying on a raised cot, with the bottom of my shirt rolled up and the top of my pants rolled down. Tattoo man swabbed my belly button with alcohol, pinched it a few times and then raised what looked like a giant darning needle.

Both Amanda and Mel sucked in their breath. I closed my eyes.

The needle felt like an icicle going through my skin, but it was over surprisingly quickly. Within five minutes I was standing at the counter, listening to instructions about rubbing alcohol.

"I can't believe you did that," Mel and Amanda said at the same time as the door to the tattoo parlor banged shut behind us. Mel looked entirely shocked. Amanda looked impressed. I thought both reactions were equally enjoyable.

Chapter Eight

I slumped into my chair at school the next morning. I could think of a hundred reasons that school should start in the afternoon. Amanda caught me yawning and did an exaggerated imitation, displaying her tonsils and her usual wad of gum.

"I slept in, okay?" I grumbled. I'd skipped breakfast, too, grabbing an orange juice at the corner store on my way to school. It wasn't helping to keep me awake.

In fact, the only thing keeping me awake was the neon yellow glow of Dodie's shirt. The more I looked at her, the more she annoyed me. It was bad enough that the entire school population called us speds. Did she have to dress like a sped? Did she have to smile at me every morning like a puppy dog, hoping I would pet her? Did she have to hand in all her assignments on time?

Her latest outfit was the worst so far. Her fluorescent yellow sweater with its drawstring top was paired with green cords — the kind that made that horrible *swish, swish* noise whenever she shifted in her seat. She looked like a 1970s lounge act.

The worst part was the blank look on her face as Ms. Samuels came in and began writing word lists on the board. Dodie's eyes were vacant, like she was watching some secret movie in her own head. It was because of her that kids like Amanda and me got such a bad rep. The more I thought about it, Dodie was the worst part of being in this class.

Maybe Amanda was thinking the same thing. She waited until Ms. Samuels wasn't watching, then she kicked Dodie under the table. Dodie flinched but didn't say anything. A couple of minutes later, Amanda kicked her again. This time Dodie pulled her chair away from the table.

Ms. Samuels turned around. "Dodie, pull your chair in and write these down, please," she said.

Amanda smirked and I grinned at her.

I looked again at Dodie's hideous yellow shirt and then at the half-empty orange juice container I'd brought for breakfast. The next time Ms. Samuels turned to the board, I gave the container a swat and it went flying across the table and into Dodie's lap. She yelped.

Ms. Samuels jumped, sending a streak of chalk across the board.

"I'm so sorry," I said, jumping up.

"What's going on here?"

"An accident," I said. "I'll run for some paper towels."

Escaping into the empty hallway, I felt wide-awake for the first time all morning. It was the same feeling that I'd had in the mall. For a minute I felt smarter than anyone else—Dodie, Ms. Samuels, the store clerks.

The feeling lasted all the way to the bathroom, where I grabbed the whole roll of paper towel. When I got back to the classroom, Dodie was gone.

"She's gone home to change," Ms. Samuels said, looking at me with a hint of disapproval. Was it because of the interruption, or did she know I'd spilled the juice on purpose?

"Wipe off the table and sit down, please. Let's try to focus," she said. She didn't even thank me for the paper towels.

In art class, Mr. Spectacles loomed over me as soon as I arrived.

"We missed you yesterday, Miss Hallard," he boomed. "Virgos are supposed to be punctual. Responsible. Par-ti-cu-lar," he said, tapping his ruler on the table with every syllable. "I don't suppose I was wrong about you? You're not really an Aquarius are you?"

I shook my head and dug in my pack for my sketchbook. When I pulled out my assignment, his eyes brightened.

"Ah. Very nice. Very nice, Miss Hallard."

I had drawn the back of Ted's head, big and round, in the foreground of the picture, with his basketball hoop in the background and the basketball in the air partway between. I was pleased with how it had turned out, although Ted had said that he wanted to be wearing number 34 next time—Shaquille O'Neal.

Mr. Spectacles didn't say anything to the rest of the class. Instead, he turned to the blackboard again and wrote "Inclines and Declines" at the top. Our new assignment was a landscape scene showing a road with both a dip and a curve.

I was feeling better after art, but it only lasted until Amanda caught up with me in the hall.

"Check out the loser gear," she said immediately, meaning my shoes. True, I'd thrown on my oldest runners that morning, but what had I done to deserve Amanda nitpicking at me?

"Is something wrong with you today?" I asked her.

"Is something wrong with you?" she snapped back.

"I asked first."

She sighed dramatically, sending her hair fluttering off her forehead. "I'm just hyped up. My foster mom's meeting with my case worker today."

"Why?"

"Some dope about me not attaining my full potential. It's like she thinks I'm secretly a genius and I'm hiding it from her."

"But that's good, isn't it? That she thinks you're smart?"

"Whatever."

"Hey, Sped!" At the word, our heads snapped up to scan the hallway. It was one of Brad's friends, but he wasn't talking to us. He was walking half a step behind Jaz, practically stepping on his heels. I could see Jaz clench his fists, but he didn't turn around.

"Hey, Sped!" he said again. Jaz didn't respond.

"That guy had better watch it," Amanda said softly, sounding somewhat entertained by the situation. "He doesn't know what Jaz can—"

As Stud Boy made a grab for Jaz's sleeve, the hallway seemed to explode into action. Jaz whipped around, fist already pulled back and plowed one into Stud Boy's face. Stud Boy went half flying, half stumbling backward until he rammed into Amanda and me. We pushed him off us and he dropped to his knees. He looked like he was clutching his nose.

"What's going on?" A teacher appeared, eons too late, as usual. Soon Jaz, Amanda and I were all being herded toward the principal's office. We flopped into orange plastic seats by the front desk, and the teacher disappeared inside.

"Nice going," I muttered to Jaz.

Amanda, surprisingly, leapt to his defense. "Come on. What was he supposed to do? He ignored it for a while. But that guy definitely deserved to be slugged."

"He did deserve it," I admitted. For a second I thought Jaz actually smiled at us. That was all he had time for, though, because another teacher ushered in Stud Boy, a piece of gauze pressed to his nose. They disappeared into the office, and a moment later the three of us were ushered in as well. We stood crowded around the expanse of oak desk.

"It was like they planned an ambush or something," Stud Boy was saying, his voice slightly muffled by the gauze. "I was walking along when this guy spun around and attacked me. The other two were waiting behind."

"That's crazy!" Amanda protested.

The principal turned cold eyes toward her. "You'll be given your chance to speak."

But we weren't. Or at least, by the time we got to talk, it seemed as if Stud Boy had already convinced everyone. Then Amanda and I talked over top of one another, and Jaz said nothing. He just stood there glaring, as if he might "attack" again at any moment.

We were shuffled back to the orange chairs to wait. Eventually Amanda's foster mother turned up. They disappeared into the office, then left. Amanda gave me a hidden wave on the way out.

Next my dad showed up, looking grim, and we got our turn in the office. The principal said that since they weren't absolutely convinced of my direct involvement, I would be given two weeks of lunchtime detention instead of a suspension. I was to consider myself on probation. Any further incidents would mean immediate expulsion.

Jaz was still alone on the chairs when Dad and I left.

If I thought the worst was over, I was wrong. As soon as we were in the car, Dad turned to me, his lips pressed together and his eyes intent, as if he were trying to see into me.

"Why would you do this sort of thing?"

"Dad, I had nothing to do with this. Honestly."

"Violence isn't going to solve things. You should know better than that."

Suddenly it was all too much. There was no use trying to convince these people —even Dad. They were already convinced that I was going to end up a convicted felon. I blew up.

"Yeah? What's going to solve things then, Dad? Should I solve things like you do, by saying nothing? If that worked, Ted and I wouldn't be moving into Mom's apartment, would we? Don't tell me how I should deal with things when you can't deal with anything!"

He was quiet after that—typically. When we got home, I went straight to my room, slammed the door and stayed there.

Chapter Nine

Our morning classes were cancelled for an assembly. I was following Amanda up the bleachers when someone shoved me. I spun to find Brad grinning at his posse.

"Oops," he shrugged, swerving past me and up to the highest row. I glared at his back and slid in beside Amanda.

Principal Harris adjusted the microphone with an ear-torturing squeal.

At our last meeting, I was too mad to even look at him closely. Now I saw that he was young to be a principal, with downy fuzz over the top of his head as if he were just starting to go bald. He looked like someone ordinary, from a Father's Day commercial. I could picture him with his family, jogging along the road as his son pedaled a bike beside him.

Mr. Harris finally got organized in the middle of the gym and began making announcements. There was going to be a school-wide food bank drive. The music teacher was starting a grad choir for the grade twelves. And the smoking ban on school property was going to be enforced, effective immediately. This drew groans from the few stoners who hadn't skipped the assembly.

The grade eight band played its newest achievement, a piece that should have been used to torture prisoners. A community nurse talked about hepatitis and the increased risks among young people. Then some drama students started preparing for a skit.

Bored, I flipped open my notebook. Ted had circled my mistakes and I hadn't had time to correct them.

Amanda nudged me. She hates homework, so I figured she was just hassling me about doing mine. Then she nudged me again. When I looked up, Ms. Samuels was standing at the bottom of the bleachers staring up at us.

"Pay attention," she mouthed, tapping her ear in teacher-like fashion.

I closed my book obediently and turned my attention to the skit. The set was a false wall painted with bricks and white ovals.

"Are those supposed to be urinals?" I whispered to Amanda.

She nodded, wrinkling her nose. "Gag me."

The plot was fairly obvious. Cool guys were hanging out smoking. Dweeby guy entered. Got his head flushed in the toilet. Got punched a couple of times in the stomach. Got left behind as cool guys sauntered out. Then— big surprise—the students led a discussion about bullying and how to stop it.

Except that no one in the bleachers would participate, so it wasn't much of a discussion.

I had a brief moment of panic as we filed out of the gym and back to class.

"Did Ms. Samuels see me get pushed?" I whispered to Amanda.

"You got pushed? When?"

"Brad pushed me when we were climbing the bleachers."

"How could she have seen that? There were a thousand kids around us."

"Did she see the scene with Jaz in the hallway?"

"No idea. And why would it matter?"

"I just thought maybe that was why she wanted us to listen. Because we got bullied."

"Hazard, are you totally losing it?" Amanda answered, popping her gum as usual. "You only get bullied if you let yourself get bullied. And we're so far from that end of the food chain that we can't even see it from here."

I shrugged, relieved. Of course Ms. Samuels hadn't seen anything. Teachers are always telling you to listen at assemblies.

"I've been thinking about Brad," Amanda said, looking at me sideways.

"Thinking about wiping that smirk off his face?"

"More like thinking about dating him," she winked at me.

I almost choked.

"Come on. He is hot. As in model-quality hot."

"First, that would be like dating the devil," I spluttered. "And second, there is no way—NO WAY—that Brad would date a sped."

Amanda chewed hard a few times, considering. "He might date a sped who puts out," she said.

"I'm signing you up for a mental institution."

She shrugged. "I don't think I'll be a sped much longer."

"What?" At the thought of Amanda leaving me alone in that classroom, my insides turned into spaghetti. "Where are you going?"

"Into regular classes. I told you my foster mom has decided that I have hidden potential.

After that scene with Jaz, I convinced her that you were all bad influences."

My jaw dropped melodramatically. "*We're* bad influences on *you*? Unbelievable."

When we arrived back at the classroom, I could hear Ms. Samuels speaking. "If there's anything you want to tell me, I'm here to listen."

Amanda and I walked in to find her sitting across the table from Dodie, half reaching for her hands. She sighed like we were interrupting something, but Amanda, oblivious, flopped into a chair. I dumped my books on the table, and Ms. Samuels stood and started writing the lesson of the day on the board. Rob was already there, rocking silently as usual. Jaz's chair was empty—he'd been suspended for a week.

When I got home from school, I found a locksmith's van in front of the house. A man was working on our front door. My dad was in the living room, looking at a blank space along the wall where the camelback sofa used to be.

"What's going on?"

"Your mom's moved the rest of her things to her apartment," he said.

"She's taken the sofa?"

He nodded, still staring at the impressions the furniture feet had left in the carpet.

"And you're locking her out of the house?"

He finally turned to look at me, squinting a bit as if deciding how much I could handle.

"I told her she couldn't have you."

"Are you serious?"

"Did you want to move?" he asked, suddenly confused.

"No!"

"Well, your stuff is staying here. She could ask for a custody hearing, I suppose."

"What would happen then?" I asked.

"As long as both of us are fit to raise you, then I think the judge would ask your opinion on the matter. You and Ted are old enough to decide where you'd like to live."

It felt strange for Dad to be talking to me like an equal, answering my questions so seriously. I turned to leave, but then thought of one last thing. "Aren't you supposed to be at work?"

"I took the afternoon off."

I couldn't remember my dad ever taking time off before.

"Just to change the locks?"

He looked slightly sheepish. "Your mom has strong opinions. It's always seemed easier to let her have her way. But I didn't want you two coming home to find your things gone."

I nodded, feeling suddenly proud of him. "Thanks."

This time when I turned to leave, he stopped me. "We're going to need a new couch."

He looked so serious that I almost laughed. "Dad, we've needed a new couch since the ice age. The brown one was ugly and the new one was embarrassing. It would almost be less embarrassing if we sat on the floor for the rest of our lives."

"Well, since you apparently have such refined taste, I thought you could choose one." He pulled his wallet out of his pocket and extracted a pile of bills.

"I'm suddenly the home décor expert?" I asked, eyeing the cash.

"You could at least suggest a color."

"Red," I said immediately.

"Not a chance," he answered, grinning a bit.

I looked at the room. The beige walls weren't really that bad, especially with the disgusting seascape picture taken down. "A light to medium green," I finally decided. "Think Zen. And it would help if we got rid of those end tables and got some in pine. Or better yet, metal and glass."

Dad nodded, as if trying to imagine the new arrangement. After a minute he handed me the wad of cash. "Take this and pick something out. If I hate it, we can always send it back."

Upstairs, I dialed Mel's number with eight-hundred dollars clutched in my hand.

"I don't think so," she said when I asked her about couch hunting with me.

"What?" I blinked in surprise. I'd known Mel since grade six and she'd never turned down a shopping opportunity.

"I've got some things to do," she said coldly.

"What's your problem?"

"Well, let's see…she's average height with about a cup of hairspray in her hair and a wad of gum in her mouth."

"You're jealous of Amanda?"

"I'm not jealous," she said. I heard her suck a deep breath through her teeth, as if she were trying to stay calm. "I just don't know who you are anymore. A month ago I knew everything about you. Then I don't see you for weeks, you blow off my calls and you take me to a tattoo parlor. It's like you've been replaced by an alien."

"Whatever." She was right, I knew. But I couldn't just hang around a new school without making any new friends.

"I'll call you some other time." She hung up and I stood scowling at the phone for a few minutes. I hadn't even been able to tell her about Dad changing the locks.

I considered calling her back and telling her, just to make her feel guilty for not asking how my life was going.

I didn't. Instead I stuffed the money in my wallet and headed downstairs to make grilled cheese sandwiches for dinner. Dad had been trying to cook and was coming closer to killing us every night. If I started early enough, maybe he wouldn't invent any new dishes.

Chapter Ten

It didn't take long for Mom to find out about the new locks. Walking home from school on Monday afternoon, I could hear her voice from two houses away. I wasn't sure if I should hurry or turn around and run in the other direction.

"You listen to me, young man," she was screeching as I approached the driveway. Ted was standing in front of her, hunched into an oversized sweatshirt. He still had his backpack on and the front door was closed.

"You give me that key," Mom continued. "I'm still a part of this family, and your father has no right to shut me out of the house. This is no time for you to start playing favorites, Theodore Hallard."

Ted didn't react until she used his full name, which he hates. I saw him cringe. I was cringing too, thinking of all the neighbors watching this scene from behind their blinds. I could just imagine the old woman across the street peering out her living room window with her chin jutting out and her nose wrinkled all the way up to her eyebrows. Soon she would be out in her yard, pretending to garden and really just waiting for a chance to say, "In my day we didn't air our dirty laundry on the street."

Mom still hadn't seen me. I seemed to be frozen in place at the bottom of the driveway.

"Well?" she hissed at Ted. "What's it going to be?"

If I were him I would have been bawling, but Ted didn't even blink. Maybe he was playing his alien video games in his head.

Whack! Mom slapped him, hard, then swiveled on her spike heels and stalked down the driveway toward her car — and me. I was still frozen. She didn't stop, though. She just walked right past me, got in her car and squealed away.

My feet suddenly free again, I walked up the driveway to where Ted was still standing.

"Thanks for your help," he said bitterly, rubbing his cheek and glaring in the direction Mom's car had gone.

"You didn't have to stand here and let her scream," I told him. "You should have told her to get lost."

Ted opened his mouth to defend himself, then snapped it shut, jerked his key out of his pocket and let himself in the house.

"You get lost," he said, slamming the door in my face.

I should have followed him in to apologize. Instead I stepped into the backyard where the neighbors couldn't see me, threw my bag on the porch steps and burst into tears. Big, sucky, little-kid tears.

It wasn't because Ted told me to get lost — which had happened about a million times before. It was because of Mom yelling, because of the smack of her hand hitting Ted's face. The sound rang in my ears like an echo. It was an echo. Amanda's hand had made exactly the same sound earlier that day when she slapped Dodie.

This is how it happened:

When I'd walked into homeroom, Rob was at the end of the table, in his own world as always. Dodie was standing with her shoulders hunched and her arms folded over her chest. Amanda was facing her, standing too close.

"Look what Ms. Dodie Doorknob has on today," Amanda sneered.

"Nice shirt," I said, raising my eyebrows. It *was* a nice shirt and it actually fit her. Maybe she'd taken my advice and started buying her own clothes. Maybe she shouldn't have taken my advice, because the shirt had obviously caught Amanda's attention.

"Probably stole it," she said, leaning closer. Dodie took a step back.

"I don't steal things," Dodie whined. "I wouldn't do that."

"I wouldn't do that," Amanda echoed in a singsong voice. "I wouldn't do that."

I threw my books on the table and walked over to finger the sleeve of Dodie's shirt. "It's just polyester. She probably picked it up at the thrift store."

I wasn't really that mean. Not as mean as Amanda was being. But Dodie's lip started to quiver and she hiccuped. Soon she was sniffing and wiping tears and snot off her face.

"You're getting it dirty," Amanda teased, grabbing at a sleeve. She caught the fabric with one of her rings. The tearing sound seemed loud in the classroom.

Dodie squealed as if she'd been attacked. I could tell her sobbing was making Amanda angrier.

"It's not worth it," I said warningly. "And Ms. Samuels is going to be here any second. Just leave her alone."

Amanda looked at Dodie once more, looked at me and rolled her eyes. "I can't handle this many dorks in one room. This is my last day here. Just came to collect my books. No more slumming with the speds for this chick."

Dodie kept sobbing. She was seriously annoying. I could tell Amanda was ready to pounce again. I tried to make her stop.

"Will you get over it? It's a shirt. The world is not coming to an end."

She ignored me and sniveled louder. Amanda stepped closer again.

"Hello? Earth to Dodie? It wasn't even that nice in the first place. Nice compared to your cardigans maybe, but let's not use that as a common fashion denominator, okay?"

Dodie didn't look up, just stood there hiccuping. Then she was bawling and pretty soon sobbing big, messy sobs. I could tell that the more she acted like a baby, the more it made Amanda mad. Soon she was going to be wailing so loudly that the whole school would turn up in our classroom. Then Amanda slapped her. Hard.

She jerked backward and her eyes popped wide open. She stopped crying, though. For a minute she stood absolutely still. Then she turned and ran from the classroom.

My eyes followed her out the doorway —and found Brad. He was stopped in the hall outside, obviously soaking in the scene. Amanda saw him too. She immediately gathered her books and sashayed by me.

"Like I said, I'm done with this loony bin. On to bigger and better things." She didn't stop to acknowledge Brad on her way out, but I could see his eyes follow her down the hall.

When Ms. Samuels finally arrived, Rocker Rob and I were the only ones left in the room.

Chapter Eleven

Dodie wasn't at school on Tuesday. Or Wednesday. Ms. Samuels asked about her, but I shrugged. Amanda wasn't there to answer.

"How should I know?" Jaz scowled, newly returned from his week off.

Our class was actually more peaceful without Dodie. I knew that if I looked at her, I'd feel guilty for not stopping Amanda. I mean, she was unbelievably annoying, but

Amanda had taken things too far. At least with both of them gone I could put the entire incident out of my mind. Besides, I had to concentrate — I had an essay due for history. Ms. Samuels had already read a first draft, and she was helping me rewrite it paragraph by paragraph.

"Think of each part of a paragraph like a part of a hamburger," she said, drawing a giant burger on the board. As if on cue, Jaz's stomach growled. I couldn't stop a giggle and even Ms. Samuels smiled.

When she turned back to the board, she started drawing arrows to her illustration. "The top half of the bun is your topic sentence," she said. "That's where you tell the reader exactly what they're going to find inside." She added a few little sesame seed dots to the bun while she spoke.

"The meat of the burger is the meat of your paragraph. Explain your first sentence. Offer facts to support it."

"Your conclusion," she said, "is the bottom of the bun. This is where you summarize what you've said."

At some point, without realizing it, I had started to like Ms. Samuels' class. I mean, I still tried to duck into the room without anyone seeing me, as if I were visiting a sexually transmitted disease clinic. (Not that I ever have.) Once inside, though, things were starting to seem more achievable.

She might not have been a sped anymore, but that didn't stop Amanda from turning up at my locker after school. She was just in time to find me contemplating the eight crisp hundred-dollar bills in my wallet. I took one of them out and waved it under her nose.

"A little shopping?"

Her eyes goggled and she tried to grab the bill. "When did you win the lottery?"

"This isn't for me. It's for a new couch," I told her, pulling the bills out of her reach. "I can spend up to eight hundred dollars and we've decided that it should be green."

Amanda groaned. "Eight hundred dollars to spend and you have to buy a couch? It couldn't be jewelry?"

Keeping an eye out for the security guard who'd chased us before, we strolled into the department store at the mall and made our way to the fifth floor — home furnishings. Amanda immediately stretched out on a three-thousand-dollar black leather sofa, calling, "Bring me a martini, will you, dahhling?"

Ignoring her, I wandered through the displays. Each couch was surrounded by its own living room — rugs, end tables, lamps, TVs. I could imagine a family of four squishing onto the big plaid couch to watch sitcoms, or a group of elderly women having tea, perched on a set of flowered sofas.

Amanda found me again just as I was testing a model that I liked. It was pale green velvet, squishy enough to be comfortable but not squishy enough to swallow me.

I stood up and, after being ignored for a few minutes, managed to wave a sales-clerk over.

"I'd like this one."

"If you can give us fifteen percent off,"

Amanda said, elbowing in front of me. "It's a bit over our budget."

I gaped at her, and the clerk cleared his throat nervously. Amanda looked at him confidently until he said, "I'll check with the manager and see if there's anything we can do."

"What are you doing?" I hissed at her as soon as he left.

"Trust me. You're supposed to bargain for these things."

The clerk reappeared. We both tried to look nonchalant. Like we bought couches every day.

"It looks like this item may go on sale in a few weeks. I can give you an early discount of five percent."

Amanda made a dissatisfied sound.

"We'll take it," I said, "if you'll include these two lamps in the price."

Twenty minutes later I walked out of the store with a receipt, a warranty and forty dollars and change still left over. The couch (and lamps!) would be delivered in two to three days.

"Come on, that was way too tame. One little adventure before we leave the mall…" Amanda teased.

I shook my head, too pleased with my purchase to risk any adventure. "I've got to head home. Thanks for your help though, Master Bargainer."

"Booorrring!" She called after me across the parking lot.

When I got home, Mom was standing on the front walk again. Not yelling this time, just tapping her foot impatiently. Ted stood with his back to the door, arms crossed over his chest.

Mom looked relieved when she saw me. "Listen, I don't want his key and I don't want inside the house. I just came to see if I could take the two of you for coffee."

"Like we're going to believe that," Ted mumbled.

Mom ignored him, appealing to me instead. "You can't just lock me out for the rest of your lives. You don't want to move in with me. I get it. But at least come for coffee."

I looked at her closely, my eyes narrowed. "You're going to have to be nice to me the entire time," I said.

Her lips narrowed into a thin line, but she nodded.

"Excessively nice," I said.

She nodded again.

"I can't believe you're agreeing to this!" Ted spit, looking at me as if I was crossing enemy lines.

"Look, you stay here and wait for Dad to come home," I told him. "Think of this as a scouting mission. Like in your video games. If all is safe, maybe you'll want to go next time."

He rolled his eyes at me and opened the front door. Then he slammed it closed behind him.

When I got home, he was waiting in the hallway for me, tapping one foot and looking very much like Mom had earlier in the afternoon. I could hear Dad doing dishes in the kitchen.

"So?" Ted demanded.

"So it was okay. I mean, the whole apartment looks like it sprouted from the pages of a magazine. It could use a few of your dirty little fingerprints."

He still looked suspicious. "Was she nice?"

"She was," I assured him. I didn't tell Ted that Mom had known about the fifty dollars that I took from the dresser. She had talked to me somewhat nicely about it. Once I promised her that I wouldn't grow up to be a criminal, she had seemed surprisingly cool. Maybe actually making the leap and getting her own place had relaxed her a bit.

I grinned at Ted. "After I made her repeat her promise to be nice, I showed her this." I flashed my new belly button ring at him.

Ted's eyes grew round. "You got…" he started to yell. Then I put a hand across his mouth and tickled him until he promised not to tell Dad.

It had been an amazingly good day— one of the best that I could remember. Even Dad's dinner was edible.

Chapter Twelve

I knew something was wrong as soon as I walked into the school on Thursday morning. The homeroom bell was still five minutes away, but the halls were quiet. Clusters of kids stopped talking when I walked by, their eyes following me.

I went to my locker and rummaged for my books, trying to figure out what was going on. When I didn't hear anything, I made my way to Amanda's locker. She saw me coming and grinned wickedly.

"Got arrested last night."

"You what?"

"I stayed at the mall and tried to lift a pair of earrings."

"And you got arrested for that?"

"That security guard has a baton up his ass," she said, not looking at me. "He went on and on about lack of respect, how I was going to grow up to be some hardened criminal, blah, blah, blah. If the cops hadn't arrived I might have puked on his polyester pants."

"What did they do?"

"They took me to the station and called my foster mom. Then I got another speech about disappointing people. Apparently the store is still deciding whether to press charges."

"Does that have anything to do with people acting weird this morning?"

Amanda raised one eyebrow quizzically. She didn't have to say anything—I knew it was a dumb question. The moods of the student body were not exactly governed by Amanda's criminal record.

"People are acting weird?" she asked, only half interested.

Before I could answer, the bell rang.

"Hey, guess who called me last night," Amanda asked as I turned to go to class.

I looked back.

"Brad. He thought I might want to hook up for coffee."

The world was getting stranger and stranger. And I still hadn't figured out what was going on in the school. When I got to class, Jaz, Rocker Rob and I sat waiting in silence until Ms. Samuels walked in.

If she weren't a teacher, I would have thought she'd been crying. Her eyes were rimmed with red, as if she hadn't slept.

"What's going on?" I asked quietly.

"Dodie Dunstan died last night," she said.

Strangely, my first thought was that Dodie had a last name. Other than Doorknob, that is. Dodie Dunstan. Was that how you talked about a dead person? You used her full name?

Ms. Samuels' voice caught, but she continued. "The police don't suspect foul play."

"That means…" Jaz said.

Ms. Samuels nodded.

"That means what?" I asked, confused.

"She offed herself. Suicide," Jaz said, turning his intense stare in my direction for the first time all morning. He pursed his lips, considering. "She seems like the pill type to me. She wouldn't want to see blood."

Ms. Samuels looked like she wasn't sure how much to tell us, but eventually she nodded. "It was an overdose."

"Did she leave a note?" Suddenly all I could think of was my lipstick graffiti on the bathroom mirror. It burned neon red in my head.

Ms. Samuels shook her head. "They haven't found a note. Classes are cancelled for the rest of the day. There are grief counselors available in the gym, the auditorium and the office. I think everyone should speak with one."

Jaz was practically out of the classroom before Ms. Samuels finished speaking. I followed slowly, though with no intention of visiting the counselors. What would I say? We were so mean that it killed her?

The funeral was on Monday.

I had spent the weekend cocooned inside the house, watching TV from the living room floor until the couch was delivered on Saturday afternoon. Then I watched TV from the couch.

Amanda called five times. Ted took messages for me. I think she swore at him the last time she called, but he didn't tell me that. Just said, "You should call her soon. She's starting to sound a little mad." I thought about calling Mel, but she'd made it pretty clear that she didn't want to talk to me.

Dad patted my head once, which I think was supposed to be comforting. Then he left me alone.

On Monday I skipped school and arrived at the church to find the parking lot filled with other kids. Girls who would never have been caught dead talking to Dodie sobbed and clutched each other. Even Brad's posse was there. One of them was talking to a TV reporter about how "regrettable" the situation was. I glared at them as I passed. The whole scene reminded me of when Princess Di died. All of a sudden, millions of people around the world were mourning like she'd been their best friend. "You didn't even know her!" I wanted to scream. That's what I wanted to yell now, right into the news camera.

I was halfway to the stairs of the church when I saw Amanda. She was heading inside, with Brad's arm slithering around her waist.

At first I thought it must be someone else. Someone who looked like Amanda from the back. But at the top of the stairs they stopped. He murmured something into her ear. She turned toward him and I saw her profile. I saw her hand, adorned in its heavy silver rings, reach to smooth his shirt.

After that I stood in the middle of the parking lot and let everyone swirl around me. It seemed like every kid in the school was there. There were teachers, too, and people I didn't recognize. At the end, a black car purred up to the stairs and a haggard-looking woman stepped out with a little girl, a smaller version of Dodie. The woman glanced at me for a second. Then someone stepped out of the church to take her arm, and they disappeared inside. The parking lot was quiet.

I'd never been to a funeral before. Not that I went to this one. Instead I sat on the front stairs of the church, my legs tucked close to my chest and my coat wrapped tightly around me. It had rained earlier in the morning. Now it was windy and the clouds were low—one of those days that seemed dark even in the middle of the afternoon.

I could hear the hymns from inside. I heard a woman's voice, but I couldn't hear the words. What would you say in a eulogy for someone who committed suicide? She loved life? She had great hopes and dreams? Apparently not.

When I thought too much about Dodie, when I thought about the lipsticked mirror or the spilled orange juice or her ripped shirt, I felt like my chest was closing. I couldn't breathe. So I tried not to think of her at all, but she surfaced in my head like the oil slicks on the puddles in the parking lot.

I heard the scrape of wood against wood and the rustle of people rising. Before someone could open the double doors and find me sitting there, I ducked around to the wall in the shadow of the stairs. Still clutching my coat around me, I watched everyone spill slowly outside.

"Terrible," I heard the principal say to one of the teachers, shaking his head and clicking his tongue against the roof of his mouth.

"That poor woman. She looks like she's aged a decade overnight," another teacher whispered to the man beside her, nodding her head in the direction of the woman and little girl who had arrived last. Was that Dodie's foster mom? Was the girl her sister?

"Brad! Quit it!" Amanda's bright voice was out of place, a splash of color in a black-and-white film. "Shhh..." she giggled. "You're going to get us both in trouble." She skipped down the stairs, followed closely by Brad, who seemed to be trying to nibble her ear. Nibble her ear? Had I fallen asleep and ended up in some other dimension?

"Amanda," I called, stepping out from the shadows. "I didn't see you go in," I lied. I avoided looking in Brad's direction.

She stopped and looked at me coldly. "So you're back, are you? You disappeared this weekend. I guess you've rejoined the world of the living now?"

"I guess," I shrugged.

She sneered, reaching behind her for Brad's hand. "Too bad the world has passed you by." Her laugh made heads swivel in the crowded parking lot.

"Amanda," I hissed. She turned slowly back to me.

"How can you be like this? What if this was our fault?" I could feel my voice growing loud and shrill.

"Shut up!" Amanda grabbed my arm, hard. "You're not making sense. What did we have to do with it? No one kills herself over a ripped shirt. Understand?"

I nodded mutely. Brad pulled at Amanda's other hand, looking uncomfortable.

"I'm leaving. We're not going to say another word about this. Ever." She looked at me steadily for a moment to make sure I had heard her. Then she tossed her hair and nuzzled close to Brad once more.

Ducking my head, I wove quickly out of the parking lot.

Chapter Thirteen

"Don't hang up!" I said as soon as Mel answered the phone. "I know I've been a jerk."

"You have been a jerk," she said warily.

It was almost nice to have someone actually say that. Everywhere I'd gone all week I had seen people who thought I was better than I am. I got an A on the history paper that Ms. Samuels helped me rewrite. My dad was practically glowing with the news.

Even Mom called to congratulate me. Then she asked if I wanted to come for dinner on the weekend.

"I sleep at home after?"

"Wherever you'd like," she said.

"I'd like to sleep at home."

"That's fine," she said, as if we were discussing pizza toppings. "Ask Ted if he'd like to join us." Ted said no, of course, but I told him that I would serve as the advance force. (I think he understands these things better in video-game language.)

"Hello, are you still there?" Mel's voice echoed in my ear. I'd almost forgotten her on the other end of the phone line.

"Listen, I'm not hanging out with Amanda anymore and I'm sorry I treated you so badly and I hate fighting with you." I said all that in one breath, not giving myself a chance to chicken out.

She was quiet for a minute and I could almost see her biting her bottom lip, considering. "How's the belly button ring?" she asked, finally.

"I took it out. It killed whenever I did up my jeans."

Mel cracked up, and it appeared that I was forgiven.

Forgiveness seemed to be coming easily —almost too easily.

After the scene with Amanda in the parking lot of the church, I'd kept my word and not mentioned being mean to Dodie. Still, Ms. Samuels caught me after class one morning.

"We've all said things we regret," she said softly. "But Dodie's been troubled for a long time."

I shrugged, but as soon as she said Dodie's name, my eyes started to water.

"This isn't your fault," she continued, touching me on the shoulder.

I nodded and turned to go, then changed my mind. "It's not that it's my fault, necessarily," I said quietly. "It's just that I made this situation worse. Maybe I could have made it better."

"Caz...one more thing," she said as I turned to go. "I think your art teacher would like to speak with you. We're putting together a memorial display and he would like to include one of your sketches."

I knew which one it was without asking. It was a charcoal portrait of Dodie in her new shirt, ripped sleeve included. I had drawn it in the days between her death and the funeral.

I nodded. When Ms. Samuels had gone, I collapsed into a chair and plunked my forehead down on the table. My chest hurt. It was as if my throat had grown smaller on the day Dodie died, leaving only a straw width for air to pass through. Every time I managed to suck in a breath, I sucked in guilt.

"I'm a terrible person," I muttered to the table.

Suddenly I heard a chair creak. I looked up to find Rob gazing at me—directly at me. Rob never looked directly at anyone.

"I didn't know you were here," I said.

"You're not so bad. Not terrible. I think you're good underneath," he said.

Stunned, I looked behind me to see if anyone else had witnessed him speaking. There was no one there.

"I thought you didn't talk," I said stupidly. Rob looked at me for another minute, silent. Slowly, he started rocking again, his finger tapping on the table.

I repeated his assessment in my head. "You're not so bad. I think you're good underneath." Was it true? It hadn't been true lately. As I sat there, my throat seemed to open up a notch and I took a deep breath.

Maybe I could make it true.

About the Author

Tanya Lloyd Kyi grew up in Creston, British Columbia, where someone she knew once punched a hockey player, inspiring the opening scene of *My Time as Caz Hazard*. Tanya has worked as a waitress, an aerobics instructor, a newspaper reporter and a graphic designer. She now lives with her family in Vancouver, British Columbia. She is the author of *Truth, Crystal Connection, Canadian Girls Who Rocked the World* and *Fires!*